READY---SET---
ROBOT !

READY---SET--- ROBOT !

BY LILLIAN AND PHOEBE HOBAN
PICTURES BY LILLIAN HOBAN

An I CAN READ Book®

A Harper Trophy Book

Harper & Row, Publishers

I Can Read Book is a registered trademark of
Harper & Row, Publishers, Inc.

Library of Congress Cataloging in Publication Data
Hoban, Lillian.
    Ready...set...robot!

    (An I can read book)
    Summary: When robots from all over Zone One gather
to race in the Digi-Maze, a power pack mixup almost
causes disaster for Sol-1.
    [1. Science fiction.   2. Robots—Fiction.   3. Cleanliness—Fiction]
I. Hoban, Phoebe.   II. Title.   III. Series: I can read book.
PZ7.H635Re 1982   [E]   81-47731
ISBN 0-06-022345-6   AACR2
ISBN 0-06-022346-4 (lib. bdg.)
ISBN 0-06-444087-7 (pbk.)

First Harper Trophy edition, 1985.

To Julia

It was Down Time,

and Sol-1 was recharging.

His solar cap was next to him

in the sun.

His lights were off.

Only a low hum
showed he was not asleep.
"Sol-1," called his mother.
"Get in here right now
and clean up your space.
It is very messy."

"I can't, Mama-Sol," said Sol-1.
"I am recharging my solar cap

in the sun.

I am going to roll

in the Digi-Maze,

and I am going to win."

"Win or not," said Mama-Sol,

"you have to clean up.

Big Rover has not been out for days

because you lost his power pack

somewhere in your space.

You are not a very neat robot."

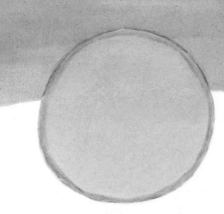

Sol-1's sister, Sola,

parked next to him.

"You'd better hurry, Sol-1,

or you'll be late for the race,"

she said.

"I am almost ready," said Sol-1.

"But I need my power pack

for the Outer Zone.

Will you get it?"

Sola rolled quickly into the house.

When she came out,

she did not have the power pack.

"It is not on your shelf, Sol-1.

Where is it?" she asked.

"I think it is under my dock,

next to my Frisbee," said Sol-1.

Sola rolled into the house again.

She looked under the resting dock.

There was a baseball,

a Space Race game,

and two dream disks.

There was a stamp album,

half a bottle of glue,

a video screen,

and a butterfly net.

Under the butterfly net,

Sola saw a power pack.

She came back outside.

"I did not find your Frisbee, Sol-**1**,

but here is your power pack.

It is sticky.

I think some glue

spilled on it."

Sol-1's red light blinked.

"I wonder where my Frisbee is,"
he said.

"Maybe it is in your game chest,
where it belongs," said Sola.

Sol-1's alarms began to beep.

• **SOLAR CHARGE COMPLETE** •

said his control panel.

Sol-1 put on his solar cap.

Sola snapped the power pack

into Sol-1's back.

"Wish me good luck," he said.

"I know you will win," said Sola.

"You are the smartest robot

in Zone One."

"Will you be at the finish line?"

asked Sol-1.

"Sure," said Sola.

"I'll bring Big Rover,

if I can find his power pack.

Now hurry!"

Sol-1 rolled to the Digi-Maze.

As he rolled,

he sang a little song:

"Ready, set, it is time to roll.

Now Sol-1 is in control.

Flashing lights and spinning wheels

make me know how winning feels.

Ready... Set... Roll!"

Friends from all over Zone One
were waiting to roll.

There was Fax—a big, thin robot.

His lights were blinking on and off.

Next to Fax was Arla.

Her control panel shone in the sun.

"Nice controls," said Sol-1.

He blinked his green light

and lifted his solar cap.

"Nice hat," said Arla.

"It may look flashy," said Fax,

"but there is no sun

in the Outer Zone.

Your solar cap

will run out of power there."

"That is why

I have my power pack," said Sol-1.

"Who else is rolling?" he asked.

"Well," said Arla,

"here come Ming[1] and Ping[2].

"And there's
that new robot,
Micromax.

And Rocko is here, too.
He has a built-in jukebox.

And over there is Super Scan,
with his X-ray vision."

"ROBOTS READY,"

announced

the Remote-Control Referee.

The robots lined up.

Sol-**1** moved between

Arla and Fax.

"ON YOUR MARK,

GET SET, ROLL!"

The robots zoomed around

the first corner of the maze.

Fax rolled ahead.

Then Arla passed Sol-1.

"Hurry up, Sunny boy!" she called.

She disappeared into

the Spectra Zone.

But Sol-1 was not worried.

He began to sing a little song:

"They can roll and they can spin,

but Sol-1 is sure to win.

Being smart is half the fight—

I know how to roll this right.

Roll…Spin…Win!"

He rolled into the Spectra Zone,
where bright 3-D shapes floated.
He rolled through some of them,
but others were solid.
Some burst into shiny sparkles
or exploded into silver bubbles.

Fax and Arla

bumped into the Spectra Forms.

They began to spin in circles.

Sol-1 tried not to hit

the moving shapes.

Super Scan pulled up beside him.

"I can see through the Spectra Zone

with my X-ray vision,"

he boasted.

"I can see through the Spectra Zone

with your X-ray vision, too!"

said Sol-1 to himself.

And he followed Super Scan

around all

the floating shapes

into the next zone.

31

Suddenly,

his alarms went off.

Sol-1's control panel lit up—

• DANGER ALERT •

In front of him

Super Scan hopped around wildly.

Beams of light zigzagged at him.

Super Scan jumped faster and faster.

"We are in the Laser Link Zone!"

thought Sol-1.

"Those beams are moving

as fast as light."

• ALERT • ALERT • ALERT •

blinked Sol-1's control panel.

A red beam slashed at him.

Then a blue one.

Sol-1 ducked,

and a green beam just missed him.

"There is only one way out!"

thought Sol-1.

Another blue beam

zagged toward him.

This time he did not duck.

The flashing light beamed him

right out of the Laser Link Zone.

"Wait for me," yelled Super Scan.

But Sol-1 could not hear Super Scan.

Sol-1 was in the next zone.

It was dark.

It was very dark.

When he turned on his scanner light,

he could see deep craters

and huge pointy rocks.

Sol-1 rolled slowly around a crater.

"I am in the Outer Zone," he thought.

"My solar cap will not work

very long in here."

His scanner light went dim.

• ALTERNATE POWER •

said Sol-1's control panel.

Sol-1 turned on his power pack.

Suddenly, he started to shake.

He began to roll backward.

He rolled right toward the edge

of a crater.

"Something must be wrong

with my power pack," said Sol-1.

Ming[1] and Ping[2] whizzed past him.

Sol-1's scanner light went out.

He rolled sideways.

Super Scan passed by.

He flashed his scanner light

and raced off.

Sol-1 heard music behind him.

It was Rocko.

He was playing "Rock 'n' Roll Robot."

"Robot Rock, Robot Roll,"

he sang to Sol-1.

"I can't," said Sol-1. "I am stuck.

I think there is glue

on my power pack."

"I will help you," said Rocko.

He gave Sol-1 a little push

to get him started.

"*Rock-a-bye, Robot,*" he sang,

and he whizzed out of sight.

Sol-1 rolled forward.

"*Bleep . . . Bleep . . . Bleep . . .*"

His alarms went off!

Rocko had pushed him too far.

He was hanging

over the edge of a crater.

"If I fall in, I will never win,"

he thought.

He pulled himself up slowly.

Three more scanner lights

flashed by—Micromax, Fax, and Arla.

"Now they are all ahead of me,"

thought Sol-1.

"I have to get out of the Outer Zone."

He sang slowly:

"This zone is no place to park.

I do not like it—it is too dark.

If I do not use my solar cap,

I will never win the... final... lap."

"I have to get back into the sun,"

thought Sol-**1**.

Suddenly he heard a noise.

It sounded like a helicopter.

"Sit, boy! Stay!" someone yelled.

It was Sol-1's sister, Sola!

"Be a good boy now!

Stay! Stay!"

Sol-1 ducked just in time.

Big Rover flew right over his head.

His tail was spinning

like a propeller.

"Help! Help!" yelled Sola.

Big Rover dove and soared.

Sola had to hang on to his neck.

"Grab his leash!"

she called to Sol-1.

"He thinks he is a space fighter."

"I can't," said Sol-1. "I am stuck.

There is something wrong

with my power pack."

"There is nothing wrong

with your power pack," yelled Sola.

"You have Big Rover's power pack.

And he has yours!

I found your power pack

behind the disk disposal.

It was next to your Frisbee,

just like you said."

"What a mess!" yelled Sol-1.

"Big Rover is flying like Superdog,
and I am stuck here on Rover power!"

"We would not be in this mess
if you were not so messy," yelled Sola.

"Heel, boy! Stop! Stay!"

Sola and Rover flew out of sight.

Sol-1 heard a loud noise

as Big Rover crashed

into the robots up ahead.

"Robot Rock, Robot Roll,"

skipped Rocko's jukebox.

"Get that dog off my controls!"

yelled Arla.

"Pretty tricky," yelled Fax.

"Who taught this dog how to fly?"

"Bow wow!" barked Big Rover.

"BOW WOW WOW!"

"New trick or not,

he is still the same old dog,"

thought Sol-1.

"I bet if I throw something,

Big Rover will fetch it."

Sol-1 threw his solar cap

into the air.

"Here, Rover, fetch," he called.

Big Rover soared through the air

and dive-bombed the solar cap.

He brought it to Sol-1.

"Good boy," said Sol-1.

He patted Big Rover

and grabbed his leash.

"That's using your brain power,"
yelled Sola.

"Hold on tight! We're lifting!"

Sol-1 put on his solar cap.

"Watch out, robots!

Here we come!" he yelled.

"Bow wow wow!"

barked Big Rover.

They could still hear Rocko singing,

"Rocket Robot, Rock it, Roll it..."

as they flew into the sunshine.

"Heel, boy. Stay," yelled Sola.

Big Rover dived.

His nose hit the ground,

and he came to a stop.

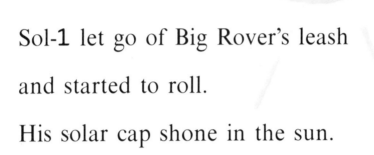

Sol-1 let go of Big Rover's leash
and started to roll.

His solar cap shone in the sun.

He crossed the finish line

on solar power.

"The winner is Sol-1,"

announced

the Remote Control Referee.

Mama-Sol was waiting

near the finish line.

She hugged Sol-1.

"You may be the winner,"

she said,

"but you are the messiest robot

in Zone One.

Come home right now

and clean up your space."

Just then the other robots

rolled out of the Digi-Maze.

Mama-Sol smiled at them.

"And after you clean up,"

she said to Sol-1,

"you can invite everybody

to a great big Digi-Party."

"Bleepity Bleep Bleep,"

yelled the robots.

"Big Rover too!" shouted Sola.

"Bow wow wow," barked Big Rover.

Sol-1 patted Big Rover

on the head.

"Yes," he said,

"because a dog is really

a robot's best friend."

And all the robots
flashed their lights
and cheered.